Where the Wind Blows

Where the Wind Blows
Helen Cresswell

Illustrated by
Peggy Fortnum

faber and faber
LONDON · BOSTON

First published in 1966
by Faber and Faber Limited
3 Queen Square, London WC1N 3AU
First published as a Faber Paperback in 1990

Phototypeset by Input Typesetting Ltd London
Printed in Great Britain by Clays Ltd, St Ives plc

A CIP record for this book is
available from the British Library.

ISBN 0-571-14425-X

For my daughter, *Caroline*,
with love

Contents

1

The Old Man of the Stile

Once upon a time there was a mill that stood
beside a lazy river called Slow. Some days it
was a fat, solid, contented mill, planted firmly
in the buttercups and with sails rolling idly in
the air. But if the wind blew, the mill sneezed
and stirred and soon it was wide awake and
a-clatter. The sails creaked and picked up
speed, they turned till the air was filled with
the rushing of the wind at work.

In the mill lived a little girl called Kirstine
with her grandfather who was the miller. He
was round and comfortable as a new-baked loaf
and had lived so long in the dusty mill that his
skin and hair were soft and powdery with flour.
He had a marmalade cat called Marigold to

catch the mice. In the meadows round the mill were fat slow-moving cows, jigsawed brown and white and with tasselled tails.

Kirstine loved the mill and the river and all the slow, lazy world that wound and stretched about her. She helped her grandfather in the mill and sewed the bursting sacks of flour with stout thread, or swept the floors and polished all the knobs.

But sometimes, on the days when the mill was fast asleep and the long hours ticked by in a drowsy sun, she would wish suddenly that the world would change and that she was far away. She wished the mill would shiver and turn to splinters and the earth rock and the fat cows go tumbledown to the river nose over tail.

'That's because you are bored,' the miller nodded when Kirstine told him one day. 'Always have something to put your hand to and the world will go well enough. You spend too long by the river dreaming.'

And that was true, for Kirstine loved to see the moorhens sail and nod in passing as they went. Or she would drop a pebble in the river and watch the water curl, or lie for hours to see the fish go by.

One morning Kirstine woke just at dawn. Outside the cock, stiff as stone, arched and sang. The dew dripped from the gates and the cold air glittered.

Tiptoe, Kirstine ran from the mill, stealing an apple from the barrel as she went.

'I shan't be home till dinner,' she told the yawning Marigold. 'The wind is away and the mill is fast asleep. You may lie all day licking your paws for all the good it will do you, but I am off to the river to find adventure.'

Her legs were wet as she waded through long grasses to reach the place where she lay to watch the river. She sniffed the night smells of the river and nettles and icy fern and root.

'Good day, Kirstine,' came a deep dark voice. 'Are you off to the river again?'

It was the Old Man of the Stile. In tattered leathers he sat on the stile, century in and century out, and watched the world and the weather. His eyes were pale and green as a sour apple, and filled with secrets to the brim.

'Yes, Old Man of the Stile,' said Kirstine, dropping a curtsey. 'I always go to the river on days when the mill stops turning. It is so quiet in the granary, and so still. I like things to move and sparkle as the river does. Sometimes, on days like this, I think I should like to run away.'

'Where to?' asked the Old Man of the Stile. He sat hunched, chin on his drawn-up knees, brown and jagged as a piece of bark.

'I don't know,' said Kirstine. She tossed her apple high in the air and caught it. 'I don't care. Anywhere in the whole wide world.'

'That's easy enough to say,' remarked the Old Man.

Kirstine was silent and a little ashamed.

'Easy enough to do, too,' he said after a little while. 'Easy enough. The hard thing is to sit on a stile, and go neither this way nor that.'

His pale green eyes flickered. He stretched out a lean hand and plucked a grass. Slowly, he raised it to his mouth and nibbled it. He

seemed to have forgotten she was there at all.

'Have you seen the wild geese?' he asked suddenly. Kirstine nodded.

'Many times,' she said. 'I often wish that I could follow them when they clap by with their necks stretched forward.'

'Do you know where they go?' asked the Old Man of the Stile.

'No,' replied Kirstine. 'No one knows. They are like the wind and go where they please.'

'No map and no compass,' nodded the Old man. 'They go on journeys and never know the endings.'

'I want to go on a journey,' said Kirstine impatiently.

'Anywhere in the wide world,' mused the Old Man of the Stile. Still he nibbled the sweet grass. 'Is that what you want? Away from the mill, away from your grandfather? You might be afraid.'

'Perhaps I might,' she said stoutly, 'but I want to go.'

The Old Man sat staring at the river.

'Come back tomorrow,' he said at last. 'You may have till tomorrow to make up your mind. But if you go on this journey, it must be without knowing the end. You must be still, like a leaf in the wind, and go where it takes you, whether you will or no.'

Kirstine stared into the sour green eyes.

'I will come back tomorrow,' she said. 'Then I will give you my answer.'

The Old Man shook himself and with a twist flung a line down into the water, ready to fish till the sun dropped. Kirstine was left looking at his hunched shoulders.

'Good day, Old Man of the Stile,' she said loudly, and went on her way, never expecting an answer.

2
Kirstine Decides

At dinner-time Kirstine went back to the mill.
It was very hot and the meadow slept in the
sun. The cows lay umbrella'd in the shade and
bees fumbled in the clover.

She pushed the creaking door of the mill and
went in. There, it was shadowy cool and so
still that she went on tiptoes. Marigold slept in
a patch of sunlight.

Kirstine shouted suddenly:

'Grandfather! Grandfather!'

There was no reply. The clocks ticked and
the pan on the hob simmered.

Kirstine ran to the cupboard and fetched the
yellow bowls and banged them on the table.
She clattered the spoons and Marigold woke,

frightened, and ran out of doors. Kirstine burst out singing as loud as she could, and did not hear the miller come downstairs.

'What's the matter?' he asked, tapping her shoulder. 'Why are you making so much noise? I was having a nap when I heard the din. Is something wrong?'

'Yes!' cried Kirstine. 'The wind is asleep and the mill is asleep and you are asleep! I wish I lived where the winds are always blowing! I don't like a world where everything is sleeping!'

'Oh, is that all?' said Grandfather, still yawning. 'You'll learn in time, that is the way life goes. Tomorrow the wind may blow and things may be different.'

'Tomorrow!' cried Kirstine impatiently. 'But what of today?'

'It's a good enough day,' said the miller. 'Where's the dinner?'

Kirstine put down her wooden spoon very carefully and turned to her grandfather.

'I'm going away tomorrow,' she said.

'Going away?' said Grandfather. 'Where to? What for?'

'I don't know where I'm going,' said Kirstine, 'and I don't really know why, except that I'm tired of spending todays wishing for tomorrows when the wind may blow.'

'Dear me,' said Grandfather, 'what a strange child you are to be sure. What did you say was for dinner?'

But a strange thing was happening. Grandfather's voice sounded faint and far away, and Kirstine did not hear what he said at all. She was listening to another voice, so near and clear that it startled her, saying 'Go where the wind blows, Kirstine, go where the wind blows.'

It was as if she were a thousand miles away, hung in space, and time stopped still. Then suddenly she was back in the dim mill kitchen, with the clock ticking loudly on the wall and her grandfather's voice was saying:

'What did you say was for dinner?'

Kirstine smiled suddenly and brilliantly.

'Here, Grandfather,' she replied, handing his bowl. And she tucked her legs under the wooden table and ate her dinner, still smiling, as if the whole familiar world of the mill was unreal and far away, because just for a moment she had glimpsed another world, one where the wind was always blowing.

After dinner she climbed to her own room and began to pack the few belongings she would need for her journey. That night before

she went to bed she found Grandfather sitting
on the wooden bench outside the mill and
watching the stars as he always did. Above
him the sails of the mill were moveless in the
quiet air and silver-edged with moonlight. It
was as if they had been sleeping for centuries.
There was such a silence and a stillness as
Kirstine had never known before.

'Grandfather,' she said softly, 'I have come
to say good-bye. Tomorrow at dawn I shall
start on my journey.'

Grandfather slowly turned his head to look
at her. He did not speak for a long while,
biding his time as he always did.

'Go, then, Kirstine,' he nodded at last. 'The
wind and the world are tugging you away. But
you will come back and find your old
grandfather and his lazy mill just the same as
the day you left them. Nothing will have
changed.'

'Except me,' said Kirstine. 'I shall have
changed.'

'When you are as old as me,' said
Grandfather, 'you will be content to let the
world go as it pleases. You will be glad that on
some days the wind blows and on others it
sleeps. My mill and I have grown old together,
and we take things as they are. Go, Kirstine,

and come back to us when you are ready.'

Kirstine kissed her grandfather and stole upstairs to her room to fall asleep gazing at the stars.

Next day she woke with the gay cock who stretched and yawned and split the glittering air. And the whole meadow was afire with sun and water in tiny licking tongues and the sky was huger than Kirstine had ever known it.

'I'm going somewhere today in the wide world,' she said with delight as she swiftly tied her bundle and tiptoed down the creaking telltale stairs.

'Good-bye, Marigold, lazy puss. Or will you come with me on my journey?'

But Marigold merely tilted an eyelid and blinked an almond eye, and Kirstine went out of the mill alone.

It was another day without a feather of wind and Kirstine ran and jumped with excitement till the dew whirled round her in a fine spray and she tasted it cold on her lips and even her arms and neck were stinging wet.

She could see the Old Man of the Stile waiting, hunched and wise, hugging himself in his tattered leathers as an owl sinks in its down.

'I'm going, Old Man of the Stile,' she called, even before she reached him. The words came spilling out and her legs tumbled eagerly towards him.

'I've made up my mind! I'm going!'

14

3
The Wicker Boat

The Old Man of the Stile was not at all
excited. He sat on a stile for that very reason.

'If you have made up your mind, Kirstine,'
he said, 'you had better get started at once.'

He took from his pocket a curious whistle
carved from a cane and blew on it, one or two
notes, not very loud, but sad and lingering. He
put it back in his pocket and they both waited.

'Like a leaf in the wind, remember, Kirstine,'
warned the Old Man. 'You must go wherever
they take you, whether you will or no.'

'They?' began Kirstine, wondering.

But then there was a sound of wild wings
beating and a rush of air and wind in that still

place. And suddenly Kirstine could feel the wind, although it was not there, and then she saw the geese, seven of them, necks green and eager, wings urgent. And she could have cried aloud with longing and delight. The geese went in a circle overhead, restless and glinting, chafing to be gone. The Old Man pointed a long finger towards the river.

Floating under the willows was a small boat made of wicker and lined with green. Trailing from the prow were two long streamers of plaited rushes, and on the side was the name *The Wicker Boat*.

'Mine?' asked Kirstine, scarcely daring to hope.

'Yours,' nodded the Old Man of the Stile. Without moving from his perch he leaned forward and with a hooked stick caught the boat and brought it in to the bank.

'Climb in,' he commanded.

Kirstine obeyed, and putting her basket and box beside her, sat on the wide seat, rocking gently on the stream and hearing the sound of the geese crying, impatient to be off.

Kirstine looked up and the jutting face of the Old Man of the Stile loomed over her. His sour green eyes were narrowed so that all of a sudden she shivered because she could feel magic as she had felt it yesterday in the dim mill kitchen.

'Remember two things, Kirstine,' said the Old Man. 'The first is that you may turn back whenever you please. You have only to tell the boat to stop three times, and the boat will turn. Do you understand?'

Kirstine nodded.

'The second,' went on the old Man, 'is that you may not speak to the wild geese, nor they to you, except in dreams.'

'Only in dreams,' repeated Kirstine, wondering at the strangeness of it. 'I will remember.'

'Go, then,' said the Old Man of the Stile. 'Farewell, Kirstine. I hope you will find what you are looking for.'

Then with a push of his long stick he sent the boat forward into midstream and Kirstine's journey had begun. She turned to wave but the Old Man was already casting out his line ready to fish all day till the sun dropped.

The boat drifted down the stream and Kirstine saw the jigsawed cows in the meadow and the old mill with its ivy coat and still sails. Above her willows fell in waterfalls of sunlit

green and soft fronds touched her cheek and neck and the sun-flecked water dazzled her till she was all a-dream and dizzied.

She lay on her back and trailed her hand and wrist in the cold water and watched through half-closed eyes the sun in golden strands among the grasses. All the time she could hear faintly the crying of the geese, but although she scanned the sky to east and west there was no sign of them.

'But they are there,' she told herself. 'For don't I hear them, and did not the Old Man of the Stile promise that they would be near?'

She knew, too, that magic was round her all the time, for the boat was moving strongly and surely as if it were rowed by invisible oars. At noon when the sun hung overhead she fell asleep and on waking she found a little basket full of cakes and fruit, which she ate hungrily.

Still there was no wind, but still the little wicker boat sailed steadily on. Now she was in a deep forest in a chill, tunnelling gloom, and the water was a depthless green and the song of birds echoed in the high trees.

As night drew on Kirstine noticed that the wicker boat was moving more and more slowly as if it were tired and seeking rest. Till at last it came to a stop among the spearing reeds and

Kirstine tied it to a willow with the long plaited ropes.

She lay on her back and looked right up to a huge sky prickling with stars, and saw for a moment the wild geese with moonlight whitening their backs, ringing above her. Then she fell asleep.

4
The Land Where the Sun is Always Shining

When Kirstine woke it was dawn and cold. Dew trembled on the fringes of her shawl, and she sat up, shaking it. There was food again in the little basket and she gobbled it quickly, eager to be off. She untied the long green plaits and the wicker boat moved away.

'Today the wind may blow,' she told herself.

By the time the sun was fully up she was out of the forest. Suddenly the world spilled with golden light and Kirstine shaded her eyes, so long accustomed to the green gloom. Blinking she looked about her.

On either side lay meadows waist-high in grass, very hot and still. In the distance Kirstine could see the roofs of a village.

'I want to go and look,' she said aloud.

Straight away the wicker boat glided to the bank and stopped. So Kirstine stepped ashore and skipped a little way, delighted to have her toes on the warm earth again. The flowers and trees were bent with blossom and fruit and the air was crowded with drifting seeds and pollen and the hum of bees.

As she drew near the village she began to see people. Their hats tilted against the sun, they were sunburnt and whistled softly as they went. They moved slowly, like people who are not really going anywhere at all. They smiled at Kirstine, slow contented smiles. Under the trees they lay in groups, toes turned up, eyes shut. The trees were hunchbacked under the weight of fruit and the air was drowsy with the scent of ripeness, of oranges, lemons and plump grapes.

In the village it was silent. The sun beat down hammer hard on bare streets and cobbles. Pigeons slept under the shadowy eaves and cats dreamed in dark doorways. Then Kirstine saw a man sitting on a bench, knee-deep in tumbling blue flowers, eyes squeezed tight shut. She went up.

'Good morning,' she said loudly. There was no reply.

'Good morning,' she shouted. The pigeons whirred with alarm and flew in a white blur. One eye opened, then the other.

'Of course,' said the man drowsily.

He looked as if he were going to sleep again so Kirstine said quickly, 'What is this place? And why is everyone so sleepy and contented?'

'This is the land where the sun is always shining,' the man replied. 'We open our palms and fruit drops into them. We sleep by day and dance by night. Why should we not be happy?'

'Does the wind ever blow?' asked Kirstine.

'The wind?' said the man. 'Never.'

And with that he closed his eyes and was asleep again. The heads of the blue flowers knocked against his knees.

Kirstine ran back to the river. The people watched her whirling legs.

'Stay, Kirstine, stay with us,' they called lazily, but she took no notice.

Pell-mell she stamped through the flowers and fallen fruit, straining her ears for the crying of the geese. The tangling grass caught at her legs as she passed, as if to keep her.

'This is not what I am looking for!' she cried. And as she spoke she heard again the calling geese and thought she felt a cool breath of wind go over her hot cheeks. Then she had reached

25

the river and she stepped swiftly into the wicker boat and cast off.

The boat moved away, but it seemed to Kirstine that now it was moving more slowly and dipping more deeply into the water. As they went she looked over her shoulder for a last glimpse of the land where the sun is always shining. Only then did she see the boy.

He was lying curled in the bow of the boat, fast asleep, his cheek resting on his folded hands. As if he could feel her gaze he suddenly opened his eyes and the next minute was bolt upright, rocking the wicker boat.

'Oh!' he said. 'Is this your boat?'

'Who are you?' asked Kirstine. 'How did you get here?'

'I'm Peter,' he answered, 'and I'm running away from the land where the sun is always shining. I meant to sail away in this boat, but I must have fallen asleep. I'm sorry now. I didn't know it was your boat.'

'Where are you going?' asked Kirstine.

'I don't know. I want to find my father. He is a painter,' he added proudly.

'My grandfather is a miller,' Kirstine told him. 'I live with him. Where does your father live?'

'I don't know,' replied Peter sadly. 'He went

away a long time ago. He said that the land
where the sun is always shining was lazy and
dull, and he wanted to go where the wind was
always blowing.'

'That is where I am going!' cried Kirstine in astonishment. 'So perhaps we shall find him after all.'

'But how do you know where to go?' asked Peter. 'No one knows where the winds go.'

So Kirstine told him the whole story of how she had longed to go on a journey and how the Old Man of the Stile had helped her. And then she told him of the wild geese and their search for the world's end, and Peter listened with eyes like moons.

When she had finished he was silent for a little while.

'And may I really go with you, Kirstine?' he asked.

'Of course,' she cried. 'And listen, I will speak to the geese in my dreams and tell them about your father. They go on so many journeys by day and by night, and hear so many secrets as they go. Perhaps they will help you and bring you to where he lives.'

So the two of them decided that this was best. And they gladly sailed away from the land where the sun is always shining, and longed for the night to come, and the wild geese.

5
The Marshes

The sun fell behind a hill. The wicker boat was idling and the first star came out. Peter and Kirstine looked at each other and smiled, sitting very still. A fish jumped and plopped in the calm water and the rings widened.

Faint and far away came the call of wild geese in flight.

'Surely,' said Kirstine, 'I am not dreaming yet?'

'No,' whispered Peter, 'I can hear them too.'

The beat of wings came nearer and lifting her eyes she saw the shadow of the geese on the sky, flying two by two with their leader before them. Twice they circled, thrice, and then down they flung like stones to the darkening river.

And as they came Kirstine cried aloud, for in the last glow of light she saw that they were linked in pairs with a fine silver chain and waiting to be harnessed to the boat. So Kirstine stooped and lifted from the water the dripping ropes and fastened them securely, while the geese cried and paddled the water and yearned forward with their long necks.

Almost believing she was dreaming Kirstine sat again on the little bench, huddling close to Peter for fear and wonder. And with a great glad shout the geese rose into the air, two by two with their leader before, and the wicker boat smoothly took the tides of air and they were afloat in the sky.

Up and up they soared until Peter and Kirstine could see the river spilt silver beneath them and fields of corn bleached white under the moon. They brushed the tops of the high trees and the boat rolled and staggered until Kirstine and Peter were pitched from side to side, gasping and clutching passing boughs like handfuls of silver straw.

The geese were silent now and nothing could be heard beyond the thunder of their wings.

And listening and watching she could never have told you where the watching ended and the dream began, for the night went like a shadow over the sun and it was morning.

'Peter! Peter!' cried Kirstine, shaking him. He blinked, woke and sat up.

'Look,' whispered Kirstine, pointing round them. 'Look where we are.'

The thinning mist shone yellow with early sun. Round them on every side were marshes, grey, flat, reflecting sky. A world without corners it lay. Curlew and piper, heron and gull were there, and the air was filled with their hungry cries.

But best of all there was a freshness, a taste of salt on the tongue and a blowing air, hardly a wind at all, but promising the wind. Kirstine threw back her head and sucked it in in great long gulps.

'Peter!' she cried, 'I can smell the sea and feel the wind!'

And Peter too threw out his chest and breathed mightily.

The wicker boat was threading the vast, bare flats, puddled with blue now that the day was growing brighter. Gulls were following with scissor-sharp cries and diving. Kirstine could

see the seven geese far away out at the very
rim of the marsh.

And suddenly, right through the pale
shafting sunlight the rain came, long and soft
and slanting on their faces. The rustling sigh of
the shower went over the marsh and stilled the
birds, piper, curlew, and heron picking fish.

Just as a rainbow began to arch they heard a
loud shout, 'Ahoy!', and looking up, saw a hut
where a hut had never been before.

'The marsh was empty,' thought Kirstine,
'and now there is a hut. This is magic.' And
she felt it, too, in her bones.

The wicker boat moved towards the hut and
Peter and Kirstine saw a thin brown man who
waited for them by the door.

'You must come in,' he told them, 'out of the
rain. I will tie up your boat for you.'

So they climbed out and gratefully entered
the hut. Inside it was shadowy and the bitter
smoke of a wood fire stung their eyes. There
were shelves of books, shelves of bottles and
piles of ropes and sailing tackle.

'Look,' whispered Peter, nudging Kirstine,
'Birds!'

There were several cages made of cane and
in each was a bird, drooping. The man entered

and told them to sit by the fire while he made some hot soup.

'My name is Jan,' he told them.

'Why do you keep birds in cages?' asked Peter boldly. 'They look so sad and drooping.'

'That is because they are hurt,' Jan told him. And as he stirred the soup and cut the loaf, he told them of his work out there alone on the bare marsh. He told how each day he took his boat, the *Puffin*, and went searching the flats for birds that were hurt with broken wing or leg, and brought them here to get well.

'And then there are the travellers,' he went on. 'I give them food and shelter when it is cold or wet, just as I am doing now.'

Kirstine went to the cages and put her hands through the bars, stroking the soft feathers of a curlew, who looked at her with soft golden eyes. And while she did so, Jan took out a pipe made from a reed and began to play. All the sadness of the marshes was in his music. It was made of birds crying and quiet sounds of water. As he played Kirstine stared at the eyes of the curlew and the spell of the marshes was on her.

When the music died away at last Kirstine heard Jan's voice saying softly:

'You must stay, Kirstine, here on the marshes. Stay, stay.'

And then she heard her own voice, as if it were a long way off, saying, 'Yes, I will stay. I will stay.'

6

A Spell Breaks

Kirstine's sleep that night was dreamless. When she woke the rain and mist had gone. The marsh glittered in the sun, the birds wheeled and speared and the song of the reed pipe still ran in her head.

'I will stay, I will stay,' she sang as she picked her barefoot way. She had forgotten the words of the Old Man of the Stile, and to the wind and the wild geese she gave never a thought. She was under the spell of the grey marshes and skimmed the salt flats lightly as a bird.

'Jan!' she called, seeing him stoop to his yellow painted boat. 'Wait, Jan!'

'Where is your friend?' he asked, straightening his back.

'Fast asleep in the hut,' replied Kirstine. 'I couldn't wait for him to wake. I wanted to be out here and to help you. This is a good life, I think I shall like it.'

Jan looked at her and smiled.

'Will you, Kirstine?' was all he said, and a faint cold breath of wind went over her and then was gone.

There was a shout in the distance and Peter came running, flying in leaps over narrow creeks and puddles.

'I woke and found you gone,' he panted. 'I thought you had gone on without me, Kirstine. But then I saw the wicker boat still tied to the post and I knew you were somewhere near. Are we going out to find birds today? May we help you, Jan?'

He too had forgotten his search for his father and the place where the wind is always blowing.

So all three of them climbed into the *Puffin* and Jan dipped his oars lightly and steered them through the maze of creeks and gullies between banks and reeds and little islands where the birds nested and flocked in storms of feathers. It was all water and sky and a clear, rinsed light.

Suddenly Jan stopped rowing and pointed a finger.

'What is it?' asked Kirstine, leaning forward eagerly. 'Ah, now I see it. Poor thing. See, Peter, his wing is broken.'

A curlew not far off was vainly beating his good wing and uttering shrill cries.

'How will you capture him?' asked Peter curiously. 'He could escape if he wanted to.'

For reply Jan drew from his pocket the reed pipe that he had played the night before. He played on it then, a strange music like the wind in the reeds and the sob of water in a creek. The curlew with the wounded wing stood perfectly still, his head tilted delicately as if he were sipping the music, tasting it on his thin tongue.

'Look, Peter,' whispered Kirstine, 'look at the other birds.'

And Peter saw that they, too, stood still as stone, enchanted by the music of the reed pipe.

Still playing, Jan stepped from the boat and lifting the wounded curlew gently under his arm turned again and the music stopped.

For a moment there was a hush, a holding of the breath. Then life ran back through the spellbound birds. The heron dipped his spindle leg again in pools and the gull blinked his polished eye, and every bird stretched and spread his feathers.

In the boat Jan passed the curlew carefully to Kirstine, who cradled it in her arms and with delight stroked the soft down of its head and neck. The bird trembled a little and lay very

still. Jan smiled over her head. The water sucked gently at the dipping oars.

Then the spell broke. A stir ran over the marsh like the first gust of a storm. The birds grew restless and took to the air in great, searching circles. Still Kirstine bent over the curlew and neither saw nor heard them.

Like giants the wild geese were striding the marsh. They filled the air with harsh cries and the waters trembled under them.

Kirstine lifted her head for the first time. As she did so, she saw the skein of geese go over and felt the wind cold on her face. She forgot the wounded curlew and her wish to stay on the marshes. She thought only of the geese and their journey to the world's end.

'I must go,' she said. 'The geese are calling me. Peter, we must go.'

He nodded. Without a word, Jan lifted the oars and drew the boat back to the hut where the wicker boat was waiting on the grey waters. As Peter and Kirstine clambered aboard, Jan took out the reed pipe and played again. But this time Kirstine was deaf to its spell. She was listening to the crying of the geese, and untied the green plaits with eager fingers.

Sadly, Jan placed the pipe in his pocket.

'So I shall be alone, after all,' he said. 'Good-bye, Kirstine, good-bye, Peter. I had hoped you would stay, but I see you must go.'

As they waved good-bye he turned and, with the wounded curlew cradled in his arms, disappeared.

'Where is he?' asked Peter, amazed. 'And where are his boat and hut?'

'Gone,' said Kirstine, 'I don't think they were ever really there at all. But for all that, if the wild geese had not come for us we might have stayed, and never reached the place where the wind is always blowing.'

7
The Marsh Lights

That evening at sunset the wicker boat did not glide to the bank for rest as usual. Fire spilt from the sky to the water, the sun dropped, darkness came, and still Peter and Kirstine were being carried through the cornerless marshes.

It was very quiet. Water splashed now and then on the sides of the boat. Sometimes a single bird would cry out in its sleep.

'Look!' whispered Peter, catching Kirstine's arm. 'What is that?'

It was a light moving, bobbing away out on the marshes.

'See,' said Kirstine, 'there are hundreds of them!'

The whole marsh seemed suddenly alive with moving lights, and here and there wide glows of blue or green swelled out and then burst like bubbles. There were soft explosions of yellow light and it whirled in shreds and splinters.

'Come Kirstine, come Peter,' voices came, whispering and hissing. 'Come, come with us!'

A soft orange light hovered in front of Kirstine and then danced off as if beckoning her to follow.

'Look, Peter,' cried Kirstine, delighted. 'Let us stop the boat and follow them!'

'No,' cried Peter, holding her back. 'Don't you see, Kirstine, they are Jack o' Lanterns and Will o' the Wisps. They vanish into the air if you follow them, and leave you lost and alone.'

A pale yellow blossom floated by and Kirstine snatched at it so that she almost lost her balance. Her fingers plucked at empty air.

'Come, Kirstine, come, come,' came the whispers, and the lights crowded nearer, jostling and weaving.

'They're so beautiful,' cried Kirstine, 'I wish I could run and catch them and play with them. Listen, how they call me. See how they throng to meet me. Help me to stop the boat, Peter. Wicker Boat, stop!'

But the boat went quietly on.

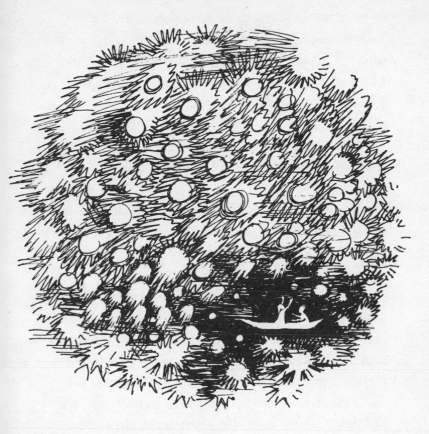

'Wicker Boat, stop, I command you!' cried
Kirstine, stamping her foot so that the boat
nearly overturned, and the thronging lights let
out a high, tangled laughter and burned more
brightly.

'Please, Kirstine, do not stop the boat,' begged Peter. 'Don't you see that the boat doesn't want you to leave? It's trying to save you from being led away by the Jack o' Lanterns and Will o' the Wisps. Come away, Kirstine, come away, please!'

But Kirstine hardly heard him. She saw only the light falling thickly now in golden flakes and the smouldering of the dark greens and blues, and she longed to reach them. She stretched out her hands to touch them as they rained past her, and thought she felt their warmth and softness on her cheeks.

'I must go, I must!' she cried again.

'Kirstine, listen!' Peter held her arm. 'Twice you have told the wicker boat to stop. If you call the third time, we shall be lost. The spell will be broken and we shall never reach the land where the wind is always blowing. We shall be left alone on the wide marsh and the lights will fade and die away and all will be lost.'

An emerald star with a blue halo floated before her.

'Kirstine, Kirstine,' came a sweet whisper. 'Leave the boat and come with me.'

'Ah!' breathed Kirstine. 'How beautiful! I'll come! I will!'

'Where are the wild geese?' cried Peter desperately. 'Oh help us, help us!'

The green star glowed and sucked the darkness in. Kirstine's eyes were fixed on it.

The wind came in a cold rush and on it came the calls of wild geese in flight, drowning the whispers of the marshes. And the wind blew the lights out as it went. They leaned and swayed, pulled out thin like candle flames, and went out.

The green star before Kirstine's eyes trembled and flickered and she heard a voice saying:

'Choose, Kirstine, choose quickly. The lights of the marsh or the wild geese. Choose, choose!'

And Kirstine felt the cold wind washing her face and hair and cried aloud with all her might:

'I choose the wind and the world's end!'

And the star cracked end to end, and fell, though there was no splash as it tumbled to the dark water. The wind ebbed and went away over the rim of the marsh. It was pitch dark and still as stone.

Kirstine and Peter, without a word, lay in their blankets side by side and went to sleep, quickly and soundly, as if they had been told to, and were obeying a voice that they never even heard.

8

Where the Wind Blows

Kirstine and Peter dreamed. They went with sleep into a world of ice and snow, into the huge silence of frost. It was as if they stood at the centre of the world for no path lay in any direction. The snow lay printless all around them.

The wild geese came into the chalky sky and they flew silently, they uttered no cry. The seven geese alighted on a single bough. It creaked and the cold air rang.

'Kirstine,' said the leader, 'you have journeyed well. Three times have you been tempted to turn aside, to forget the land where the wind is always blowing. Three times you have chosen well.'

'And you, Peter,' the bird continued, 'you
have deserved to find your father, and we will
bring you to him, never fear.'

'Thank you,' said Peter, and his breath smoked.

'After that we seek the world's end, where
only we and the wind may go. Farewell!'

The seven geese took the air and ice
splintered from their feathers in silver needles.
Peter and Kirstine were left standing at the
centre of the spokeless wheel of snow.

Then it was morning and there they lay in
the wicker boat. And the moment Kirstine
raised her head she felt the wind blowing at
last, cold and strong and salty. She saw that
the trees were pitching and the grass leaned
and shivered. The water pursed and wrinkled.

'Kirstine!' cried Peter, waving his arms,
'We're nearly there! We must be!'

Kirstine tightened her shawl round her
shoulders.

'The river is widening,' she said eagerly. 'We
must be near the sea.'

As she spoke they rounded a bend and
suddenly in front of them was the sea itself,
grey-green and restless, shouldering the land.
They could see a village on the cliffs above
them and beneath it a harbour full of bobbing
boats. Black-headed gulls were riding the wind,

scooping and soaring. Everything moved and glittered and sang in the blowing air.

'The wind! The wind!' chanted Kirstine joyfully, and her cheeks were whipped into redness.

The wicker boat sailed in by the harbour wall and the wind dropped a little and the sun burned strongly. On the quay were fishermen busy with baskets of fish. All the people laughed and sang and the golden weather-cock on the stone steeple whirled and flashed in the wind. And the wind was always blowing and making movement; boats bounced and the clouds ran along the sky, shawls flapped and the waves slapped on the barnacled wall of the quay.

Kirstine squeezed her hands tight together and almost laughed aloud because it was so careless and so beautiful.

As the wicker boat drew to the side, willing hands pulled on the green ropes to make her fast to a rusty iron ring. Kirstine and Peter stepped up on to the quayside and for a moment the ground came up and the world went steeply sideways, making them dizzy. The crowd drew round, eager and excited.

'Who are you?' they cried. 'Where are you from?'

'I'm looking for my father,' said Peter. 'And Kirstine is going to the world's end.'

Kirstine stood shyly by and people nearby nodded and winked at her delightedly.

'It's Mr John's boy,' they said to each other. And 'Look at that – come sailing in right out of the blue!'

A tall man with a brown face and shiny oilskins told them where Mr John lived.

'Cuttle Cottage, Cuttle Hill,' he told them. 'Right up at the top, next the sky.'

Peter and Kirstine thanked him and went on along the gusty quay. It seemed to Kirstine that the whole place was alive, even to the rough grey stones under her feet. An old fiddler was playing tunes, while his rags streamed about him and barefoot children danced to his music. Laughing women walked swiftly by, baskets balanced on their heads and spray showering about them.

Kirstine and Peter started up a steep cobbled street of nudging cottages. Up and up they climbed, and the higher they went the harder the wind blew, plucking their clothes and filling their mouths with air as cold as water. Right at the very top was a leaning yellow house, blown sideways by a century of wind.

'Father!' called Peter, pushing open the door.

They went inside and a gust blew in with
them, scattering papers about the room and
swinging the hanging lantern.

'Father!' cried Peter again. He banged the
door shut, so that it seemed suddenly very
quiet and still. No one came.

'He's painting,' said Peter. 'Every day he
used to paint till the sun went down. We'll find
him.'

57

Out they went and up to the cliffs. They called to each other but were deafened by the thunder of the wind and waves. Then they saw him, at his easel, sheltered behind a huge, whitish boulder.

'Father!' cried Peter. And Mr John flung down his brush and ran to meet him, his thin face shining.

'You've come!' he cried.

Then they sat behind the chalky stone and Kirstine and Peter told him of their travels, of the wild geese and the marshes and the Jack o' Lanterns. He seemed to listen, but by and by his eyes began to wander, back to his canvas and the wet, shining paints. His fingers began to twitch, and in the end he got up without a word and began his painting, as if he had forgotten they were there at all.

A white mist was rolling in from the sea when at last he put down his brushes. They walked back over the cliffs watching the lights come out below them one by one, decorating the dusk.

Kirstine had never felt so tired in her whole life. She ached where the wind had hammered her from head to foot. At Cuttle Cottage there was hot stew by the swaying lamplight and a steep climb up rickety stairs and then at last a

slow sinking into a deep bed of feathers,
sleeping even as she sank.

9
World's End

Next morning Kirstine woke early and lay for a
moment wondering where she was. She was
used to feeling the movement of the wicker boat
and seeing a tangle of leaves about her. Now
she was lying on a bed and above her were
beams decorated with cobwebs and lobster
pots. A stuffed seagull stood on each bed post.
Seeing the birds made Kirstine remember the
wild geese. She jumped up. She had not seen
them since they had spoken to her in the
dream, and she ran to the window and threw
it open.

A cold gust of wind blew in. Dawn was
breaking over the sea and the gulls were
waking and walking on the shingle or

screaming from the chimney pots of the
cottages below. As she watched, the seven
geese came into the hyacinth sky, lit with sun
and cutting the morning like arrows. They flew
down and alighted on the black rotting wood
of the jetty.

'Soon they will be gone,' thought Kirstine,
'off to the world's end. I must say good-bye.'

She turned to the tumbled bed and seized her
shawl and leather shoes. She ran down the
curving stairs and through the painter's tackle
and sleeping pictures and out into the empty
street. A window banged open above her and
first Peter's head appeared, then Mr John's.

'Kirstine,' cried Peter, 'where are you going? Wait!'

'I'm going to see the wild geese go,' said Kirstine. 'And then I must go too. Grandfather will be waiting for me.'

'But you've only been here a day,' said Mr John. 'I thought you wanted to live where the wind is always blowing?'

'I did,' said Kirstine. 'But now I'm here and it's the end of the journey. Today the wild geese will fly to the world's end and the adventure will be over.'

'Just for a day, Kirstine,' pleaded Peter.

The wind whipped round her legs and curled her shawl around her. On it came the calls of the geese far out at sea.

'I can't,' she said. She remembered the words of the Old Man of the Stile. 'You must go where they take you, whether you will or no.'

'I must go, Peter,' she cried. 'But I shall see you again one day, I know I shall. I'll come myself, now that I know the way. I shan't need the wild geese next time. Good-bye, Peter. Good-bye, Mr John!'

And she began to run pell-mell in case she should change her mind, past the church with its whirling cock, past the lobster-pots and window-boxes of geraniums, past the shell

gardens and rows of cockles down to the gusty
quay. The wicker boat lay knocking against the
sea wall and Kirstine untied the green plaits for
the last time and climbed down. Straight away
the boat moved off, strongly and surely
threading the crowded harbour until it reached
the outer wall and the open sea.

And the wind blew, every minute it blew
more strongly until Kirstine felt as if it were
blowing through her very bones, blowing
through her fingertips, elbows, feet. She could
see the seven wild geese in a sky of white and
violet as if a storm were coming.

'Shall I turn back?' thought Kirstine, half
afraid.

But the wind was too strong, blowing through her and over her now, and when she looked ahead she saw that the wild geese were going right over the rim of the world like stones dropping.

'The world's end!' cried Kirstine in wonder. 'The wild geese have reached the world's end.'

And after that Kirstine could remember nothing, except that for a moment everything seemed to stop. Even the waves hung half-furled and the wind went out like a candle flame. Everything stopped, and there was silence.

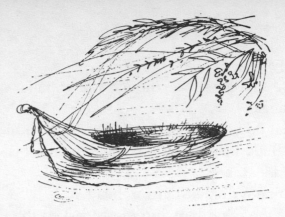

10
Home

Kirstine felt as if she had been dreaming. She
opened her eyes and a white-flowered nettle
waved across them. She could smell its
sharpness. She sat up, rubbing her eyes with
her fists.

'Well,' said a deep, dark voice, 'it's little
Kirstine home again.'

Looking up, she saw the mountainous face
of the Old Man of the Stile, with its crags and
hollows and sour green eyes.

'And did you reach the place where the wind
is always blowing?' he asked, smiling as if he
knew a secret.

'Yes,' nodded Kirstine, 'I reached it.'

'And did you see the geese fly to the world's

end?' he asked.

'Yes,' said Kirstine, 'though I only half remember.'

'What do you remember?' asked the Old Man of the Stile, huddling from the dew into his tattered leathers.

Kirstine wrinkled her forehead.

'Was the wind blowing there?' asked the Old Man slyly. 'Or was it very quiet? Quieter perhaps than the old mill?'

'You have been there too,' cried Kirstine suddenly. She knew now why the Old Man's eyes were brimful of secrets.

'Yes,' he nodded. 'I too.'

Kirstine climbed from the wicker boat and began to tie the long green plaits to the trunk of a willow.

'No,' said the Old Man of the Stile. 'Let it go. You won't need it again.'

'No,' agreed Kirstine. 'Next time I can go alone.'

She let the plaited reeds slide through her fingers and they dropped to the water with a soft plash. The wicker boat began to drift slowly into midstream.

'I must go to the mill,' said Kirstine, not wanting to watch it out of sight. 'Grandfather will be waiting. Good-bye, Old Man of the Stile.'

'Good-bye, Kirstine. Remember, I shall always be here.'

Kirstine nodded. So he would. Century in and century out, in his tattered leathers, watching the world and the weather.

She ran eagerly through the tangle of wet nettles with their bruised scents and smells of earth, until suddenly she was out in the sunlit meadow and the old mill stood there just as she had left it, half-asleep among the jigsawed cows.

And suddenly she did not care that the sails were still, because she had been where the winds were always blowing and she knew that her grandfather was right. Some days the wind would blow, on others there would be never a whisper. But somewhere the wind was always blowing and now she had it in her bones for ever.

Marigold lay curled like melted butter in the sun and blinked a narrow eye. The mill door groaned on its hinges. At the bleached table sat Grandfather, fast asleep, his powdery head resting on his folded arms. The clock ticked, the pan simmered.

Tiptoe and smiling, Kirstine quietly fetched the yellow bowls from the cupboard and filled them with the steaming broth. The dust sailed idly down the long sunbeams and the flies droned in the doorway.

Gently, Kirstine shook her grandfather by the shoulder.

'Wake up!' she said softly. 'Grandfather, I'm here!'

And he looked up and smiled as he woke, so pleased was he to see her again. And when they had greeted each other they tucked their legs under the table together and drank their broth as if nothing had ever happened.

Grandfather let out a long sigh and wiped his mouth on his sleeve.

'Ah,' he said. 'That was good. And did you go where the wind blows?'

'Yes,' said Kirstine.

'I have never been there myself,' said Grandfather. 'But it must have been very interesting. What did you say was for supper?'

Kirstine smiled.

'Kippers, I think,' she said.

And a sudden rush of wings went by out in the windless meadow.

'Yes, kippers, I think,' said Kirstine. The wings had gone and the clock on the wall was ticking again.